MISSING BLOOD

SAHANA RAVI

BLUEROSE PUBLISHERS
India | U.K.

Copyright © Sahana Ravi 2025

All rights reserved by author. No part of this publication may be reproduced, stored in a retrieval system or transmitted in any form or by any means, electronic, mechanical, photocopying, recording or otherwise, without the prior permission of the author. Although every precaution has been taken to verify the accuracy of the information contained herein, the publisher assumes no responsibility for any errors or omissions. No liability is assumed for damages that may result from the use of information contained within.

BlueRose Publishers takes no responsibility for any damages, losses, or liabilities that may arise from the use or misuse of the information, products, or services provided in this publication.

For permissions requests or inquiries regarding this publication,
please contact:

BLUEROSE PUBLISHERS
www.BlueRoseONE.com
info@bluerosepublishers.com
+91 8882 898 898
+4407342408967

ISBN: 978-93-6783-056-7

Cover Design: Shubham
Typesetting: Sagar

First Edition: January 2025

Prologue

It had been 12 years since she vanished. She had disappeared. Esta Raven was her sister and she hadn't seen her in 12 years. They didn't talk about her in the courtyard. Chatèotes did their rounds around the castle, giving an occasional nod if they saw her take a stroll outside. Aura loved going outside. Her strawberry blonde hair would sway in the wind as her arms waved freely, her rough fingers brushing the tips of perfectly trimmed grass. She could remember Esta and her dance near the Revetga lake. Aura despised herself for how much she missed her sister. Don't you remember? She was a TRAITOR. She betrayed the bloodline. She-

she- Aura forced herself to stop. She had to move on. It was good Esta was gone. She would've killed everyone. Her blood confirmed it. She was an Athkarva. A disgrace. Athkarvas were known to be dirty and impure. A great surprise to her mother and father. The Hergal and Wyrmine. No one had ever been an Athkarva with royal blood. Esta disappeared a week later. She was 15. Aura was 13. There were great searches for her. Each one ending with Esta's presence still not known. Sometimes she wondered whether they had forgotten. Equeinos came by and promised them a future with the future of Wyoming. Aura didn't fall for the assumptions they had stated. The untruths were hardly believable, especially after 12 years. There was simply no reward in hoping. So she stopped hoping. Esta was nobody- but a faint, dark shadow. A shadow waiting to be awakened.

Chapter 1

If someone wished for death, they would talk to Alok Gaudin. No one *dared* to say a word to him. He could outsmart the wisest. He worked at the *Mierchir Coast*— a private detective. Vetabelle knew him better as 'Masked Assassin'. More than not, people often believed he investigated his own kill. He had a younger brother, Giullis Gaudin. He had run away years ago, many speculating he feared his own blood brother. Alok had done the blood ritual. He was deemed *Athkarva* but even *Hergal* hesitated to confront him. The *Hergal's* daughter, Esta Raven, disappeared after being confirmed an *Athkarta*. Specialised people from

Mierchir assisted the *Hergal* and *Wyrmine* on their desperate hunts for Esta. Kai had been one of the 'lucky' few anointed with this exclusive task. The search went on for years. 4 years and 63 days to be exact. And then they gave up. She was gone.

Now, Kai was standing right outside Alok's abode. Vines crawled on the cracks of the stone bricks making up his accommodation. His father, Ralnor, had built this house using Arcane magic. Magic so powerful it could kill you with the wish of a host. All the Gaudins possessed this magic...except for Giullis. He had no power. He was an *Artcotos*- no magic being. There were only 8 non-magic beings in Vetabelle. One being Kai's mother. Kai's mother was dead. Kai realised she was now unfocused. A *sin*. She was standing outside the most feared man in Vetabelle's house. One wrong move meant death. She held the knocker. It was carved with a *Skiaumbra*. The symbol of Arcane Magic. She fingered the snake-like body of the creature, its features clearer than Vetabelle day.

"Kairini." Alok stood in front of her. He wore a dark jerkin and tall leather boots. His black robe was streaked with hints of murky grey. The hood was trimmed with fabricated gold and covered his pale, colourless face. "The name's *Kai*." She scowled. *Most* people feared

Alok. Not her. They had worked alongside each other in the desperate search for Esta. Kai would even say she was used to his alarming tactics. Alok smirked before he let her into his rather impressive residence.

His home was made up of several sections. The section Kai saw straight ahead of her must have been a corridor to a room. To the left, a marble set of stairs led down to what she presumed was a basement. A grand picture of the Skiaumbra was placed at the end of the corridor. The walls were painted grey. The floor...the floor didn't exist. Clouds of shadows drifted through the air, carrying Kai and Alok wherever they went. "Are you just going to stand there or would you like to come down with me?" Alok stared at her. His blank, grey eyes studied her face. He grinned. "You know 'Kairini' means ebullience? I'd say you're anything but." he asked teasingly. Kai tried not to push it too far with her silent treatment. Alok worked in the *Guavlepo* department in *Mierchir Coast*. An intimidating colleague with a dry sense of humour. The pair headed downstairs using the rather set of stairs. Her expectant feet awaited cold marble but were greeted by a somewhat empty step. "Shadows. Arcane magic." He said it smugly. When they arrived at the basement, Kai froze. The wall was adorned with frames, each one bearing the picture of a missing person who had been found, with small gold labels with their names and a summary of what had happened to them. The person who had organised each of the investigations to find them was Alok. Next to each of his pictures was an item. Each item belonged to the person whose image was on the wall. There was one of the council member's nieces. She had gone missing at 13 and found at 15. She had managed to get herself lost in one of the country's largest forests on a hike. Next to her framed picture was her cracked pair of glasses. The same story went for the rest of the people, and Kai knew very well no one had given him consent to take their personal belongings. He was a thief.

Chapter 2

"I know my tricks." He commented. Kai felt her blood go cold- a sensation she found, she rather enjoyed. The thrill flooded her clouded mind. *I am working with an assassin AND a thief.* "There's only one thing left for my collection... and you're gonna help me find her," Alok whispered. *Her. Estella Raven.*

Kai left his house, questioning why she had even come. The primary purpose of her visit was to inform him that she was to change departments, under the supervision of the *Hergal*. Too many appalling memories filled her when she saw her everlasting scars. They streaked her face and made secret marks, almost a maze, around her body. A maze she had never solved, and never would.

Kai crossed the arched bridge connecting Alok's house and the rest of Vetabelle. Vines grew freely on the wooden structure and the planks she walked on creaked with every step. It was the eventide of day and a soft breeze was present. Kai put up her hood and tucked her long, silvery hair behind her ears. She stroked the crossbow she hid in her trailing robes. It felt good to know she was safe.

Her ears could pick out even the slightest of sounds. The hum of the wind, the whispers of the flopures that grew wild in the woods, andnow she could hear the pattering of footsteps nearing the bridge. She didn't take out her crossbow just yet. She could listen to *his* thoughts and the pace of his heartbeat. Whoever this was, it wasn't a threat.

He was getting closer, his swift feet closing in on her. At last, she could see the man. He wore a lengthy cloak, a shade of deep Brunswick green. His head was covered in a wide hood. It was trimmed with black ribbon and dragon needlework. He wasn't meant to be here. He knew it as well. He held up a grubby finger, and his dark eyes narrowed. "Follow me..." His left hand reached into his cloak pocket. He pulled out a sharpened knife. It was a fresh kn; the blade had yet sunk into the flesh. There was no entailment for concern though, the crossbow could kill the man before he could raise his pitiful knife. His heartbeat was steadily increasing, Kai could make out. He was more anxious than her. She found that that was especially common with folk. The tip of his lip twitched, as he attempted to remark. "Follow. Please…" The despair in his voice was clearer than day.

Chapter 3

The air was stuffy and smelled of wet weather. Erle was used to it. The floor was damp and the cold, metal chair hadn't been used in a while. They were expecting visitors today. Sent a new man on the job. Personally, she found this insulting. He was young. Hardly 15. It was apparent he would rather be somewhere else. They all would. But that's not how you played the game. Trust is a curious thing. It can be built and broken like all things. But it was intangible and unpredictable. It gets built over months and years but can be broken in less than a second. It's vulnerable and weak. Erle didn't believe in trust. She was a more "see it to believe it" kind of soul. And she hadn't seen an ounce of bravery in the boy. The name was Ogtik. He was taken 3 nights ago. He showed 'potential' they said. Erle didn't mind too much. She generally preferred staying inside. It wasn't as if she had much of a choice anyway. She left the parlour room, the uncomfortableness of it wrapping itself around her. She opened the metal latch that locked the trapdoor, guarding the lab. The door was burdensome, but Erle managed to open it. The door was chiselledwith impressive figures of *Ilvremere*. As remarkable as they may be, she still had a bitter resentment towards the supposed heroes.

A wooden ladder presented itself to her. She fastened the latch as she made her way down. The lab held secrets that could rip this world apart. And in just 24 days, it could just happen. Erle didn't want it to happen of course. All she desired was to go back to her welcoming lodgings. It had been 3 *years*. She had never felt this safe *and* at risk at the same time. She had yet again no choice. She had signed away her life to them. She was all theirs.

Chapter 4

Kai didn't struggle. She knew who this was. A *dragon-trader*. More commonly known as *Dracoros*. Newspapers flashed their names. Often civilization's last resort. A desperate attempt for protection. Helpless victims soon became the Kingdom's greatest threat. But all things come with a cost, no matter what they make you believe. You sell your soul. You become trapped in an endless loop of terror and security. Quite literally a gamble of life. *Mierchir* pledged to discover the transgressor of this society. They still hadn't. Genuinely, Kai thought this of an opportunity. To finally win a battle she had been fighting for years on end. To prove herself. The *Hergal* may have advanced her to a higher post and division, but she wasn't important. Her last significant operation was 12 years ago.

The man had dark circles under his eyes, his lips were thin and scowling. His thoughts blared out into the open like a drum. He was distressed and his fingers fidgeted. Whoever this man was, he certainly didn't want to be here. Kai followed the man into a long, black Aston Martin. There was someone inside driving the car. His face was unrecognisable and covered in blood. His lengthy fingers held onto the wheel, ready to move after Kai entered the car. It was a long journey. No one spoke, though a few occasional glances from the *Dracoros* came by. She kept tabs on the direction they were going. She was hardly scared. Kai liked to believe alarmed was the lowest you could go, something that should go unpracticed. She was an investigator who had willingly let herself go along with some of Silverpeak's most wanted.

After about two hours, they reached an empty land. The door opened and the *Dracoros* stepped out. Kai did the same as the man chanted a few words.

>   *"Efridete Ineja Scarous Wxaein"*

The pair shifted into a cellar. It was dimmer than a prison cell. The air was heavy and unforgiving. She was greeted by a sinister lady, in her mid-fifties perhaps. She wore a black gown jewelled with diamonds at the neck. Black flats studded with faux gems were present on her feet. Her hair was styled into a tight, uncomfortable bun, an experience people she met felt often when they were anointed with her. She had a cold voice that sent shivers down Kai's spine. "Any trouble at all, Ogtik?" She asked, eyeing the man. "N-No ma'am. A-All clear." Ogtik said hesitantly. "Very well done. You may go now, but *you* stay." Ogtik shifted. Kai twirled her fingers, imitating the way he did to shift. She was the type of person who gathered every piece of information she could find, handy for a detective.

The lady stepped towards Kai, smirking. She had a large scar along her right arm, looking as if it had barely any medical attention. A tattoo was on her wrist, right at the place where her hand and arm connected. It was the symbol of the *Athkarvas*. A term that flooded the lonely streets of Vetabelle with fear. The ritual took place right before the feast in November. The only time the blood moon showed itself to the residents of the kingdom and the entirety of the nation. The ritual would happen a slight distance away from Vasilioroi, the Capital of Silverpeak, in the surrounding meadows. The remarkable, foreboding Kaformdi trees swaying in the wind. The ritual occurs once every year. All the people of the age of 15 would go, and see what fate their lives had to offer. The nights following November were the tensest. People wore black, often a mourningcolour, to prepare themselves for the tragedy if their loved ones were *Athkarvas*. *Fermodites* cut through your forearm and remove some blood. They used a special dagger, it was silver-engraved carved with vines and encased in ruby. The actual blade was opal, and it was bent and curved. It was truly beautiful, but Kai was sure people whose arms were being cut didn't feel the same way. Their blood was all that decided their future. *Athkaravas*- DIRTY BLOOD. *Kalospus*- PURE BLOOD. It was as simple as that. Kai always wondered why the *Dracoros* ministry existed. Who were they so intimidated by, and why? An assumption was now bubbling up inside of her. She just had so much going on in her marvellously abstract and complicated mind. Thoughts clicked into place like puzzle pieces and the ones that still didn't make sense flooded through her head like a tidal wave. It helped if she wrote it all down. She enjoyed the feeling as if the overcomplex jumble of mess were being transported into the simple body of a pen. There were still some that stayed in the back of her brain like stubborn cobwebs that refused to be dusted. They filled her mind and took over like a cyclone. They felt like a river reaching a peak, making its way to descend into a waterfall.

"Kairini Eldar Haela, we meet at last. "

Chapter 5

As confusing as this was, Kai kept her composure. To address all these problems, Kai did nothing. It was that she had met this odd lady once. An outburst in the Council meant outcasts held hostage could escape. They called it the Time of Troubles. Transgressors took hold of society. There was a pause in royal power. This lady was its leader. Juniper Morrow. She was deemed to be dead after the "Domination" fell apart. People were killed, a few of them being Kai's own mother and father. Hatred fuelled her body like never before. There was no proof of who killed her parents, but she knew it was one of the *Dominations*.

Kai had to get revenge. She was thirteen, a year after the end of the Time of Troubles. Her parents died. she was an orphan. Her grandma died a month after looking after her, with no apparent reason why. The cottage in which she used to live was sold and she slept the nights away in capable trees and lived off fruits that, by chance, were laid upon her path to seemingly nowhere. Her fifteenth birthday came and went. She was trained, quite miraculously, by the Mierchir coast. She was an apprentice for 3 long years. And then, she met Juniper. Her parents were killed when Kai was 11. In front of her own eyes. Morrow killed her family. Her cold, lifeless eyes confirmed it. Then, at the end of the Time of Troubles, she disappeared. She was then accepted dead. Until now.

Kai glared at her- the devil that stood before her. "I see a 15-year-old boy has managed to capture you. "Morrow smirked. "I allowed it. I was curious." Kai snarled.

"I'm not quite as naive as you may think, Haela. You're not curious. You're desperate. So, you can tell *Hergal* about us. Quit it, 'detective'. You aren't going anywhere." Juniper retorted. Kai kept cool. Of course, she could get out. She just needed to stay a while. She needed answers. But she wasn't sure how to get them. She got an idea. *Ask some questions.*

Kai tried to be as subtle as possible, which she found especially difficult, all things considering that this was the lady who murdered her defenceless parents. "Why did Ogtik take me here?" she whispered hesitantly. "Haela... remember your father?" Juniper questioned. This wasn't meant to happen. *Kai* liked to ask questions. Her father was still clear in her mind though. He was *magic*. He could deceive the most cultivated of minds. He made people think twice about seemingly tangible things. He created mirages that perplexed others. He was the greatest asset *Mierchir Coast* ever had. He stumped them. She had once wished to go to the *Azuraki Mountains*. But the Athkarvas infiltrated it, keeping their fatal weapons in the cracks and waterproof bombs in the *Shipati Creek*. He made it for her. Stone by stone, he built one of her dreams, all in their backyard. Her naive eyes thought it was the most beautiful in the world. Before the Time Of Troubles. When the Council was more powerful than ever before. Then it happened. It was just seven months before her parents were killed. *Murdered*. He made it for her, spending every waking moment for weeks making it. It didn't last for long. Just like her father. They were both *mirages*."*Yes,*" Kai replied softly, tears forming in her eyes. "What about your mother?" Morrow pressed. Kai put her hand up. Juniper was a telepath. And it was obvious why she was asking questions. She refused to answer them. Morrow frowned. "You won't get anything out of me," Kai said, her brows furrowing. "Oh I'm *sure* I will." Kai tampered with a gun in her robe pocket. This was pathetic. *She* was pathetic. She was in an underground prison, infiltrated by Athkarvas. A chance to learn any information about them would lead the coast to discover the whereabouts of some of the most wanted criminals. And what was she doing? Reminiscing about passionate memories regarding her long-deceased father. It was hardly surprising that Kai wasn't in a higher position. "You *are* pathetic, Haela. The revolution is happening, darling." Morrow hissed.

The revolution is happening...

Chapter 6

She could blame society, but she was society. She was part of a society no one wanted to be in. Protection was unheard of, and coming here was the closest thing. And knowing things about the Silverpeak dynasty didn't help much. Erle played with her braids, as she entered the lab. There she saw Edwin, tinkering with some old mechanics. He was the brains of the division. "Hey", she smiled, "whatcha making now?" "Morrow needs me to make a gun that shoots out nets to trap people, *apparently*." He replied. Edwin came to Dracoros the same day she did, and he was one of her favourites. He was part of a gang, desperate to get money. But they turned against him. *Attacked* him. So, he came here. "They say our visitors will have a more permanent residence," Erle announced. Edwin looked up from his complicated machinery. "Ogtik completed his mission, I presume?"

"Yes. This time, they brought someone from the Coast."

Edwin's face changed, as he turned a ghostly pale. "Why?" he whispered.

"Information."

Edwin nodded as he turned away. He walked towards a cabinet and unlocked it. He pulled out a beaker stained red and some chemicals. He twisted the lid and let the green vapoury mixture station into the beaker, waiting for a reaction. It slowly turned white, the chemical responding with the red stain. Erle assumed he was making the web.

She continued watching him stir the product, standing by for him to say something. Edwin was her only actual friend, and they had been close since the day they met. And she knew him well enough to know that he didn't say things right away.

"What if they find out about us," he said under his breath.

Erle raised her eyebrows. "Just 24 days Edwin. 24 days to make this right. Or else it'll be too late." The revolution was necessary. It made sure that the blind people of society saw that shutting away the 'imperfects' wasn't helping them. It was helping the Athkarvas. Their supposedly impure blood divided them from their higher. It was only a matter of time until more Kalospus realised why they were fighting. Fighting *back*. For the injustice that surrounded them. To create a better world for future generations. It had been over a decade since the last revolt. Erle didn't want another one. She wanted a country of peace and equality. But that was unrealistic. Erle didn't waste her time being unrealistic.

It was high time she got on with her own work. She waved to Edwin and received a gentle smile, before climbing back up the ladder to the main ground. She could hear Juniper whispering to the Coast member they had brought. It was a female. And she seemed bold. Not at all how she thought kidnapped people would behave. Suppose she wasn't kidnapped. Suppose she had a deeper reason to come here and the Dracoros just made it easy for her. But this was hard to believe. She couldn't imagine anyone wilfullycoming here to this dehumanising hub of sorrow. The only thing that separated her and their conversation was the grey barrier of cement and wall and a chilly metal door. She turned around, not wishing to dig into their business. Being involved in anything can be dangerous. She stepped carefully, calculating her paces, avoiding all the bad floorboards. You never knew when someone was underneath, concocting a fatal substance, or a weaponry unit, with spikes and katanas and staffs. At last, she reached her segment. The Research Lab- or the RL. She was the only one in this division. She often found that people would rather fight useless, defenceless mortals than work in a quiet lab with an AC. She unlocked the padlock from the large, iron door. This room held more secrets than the entire underground. She placed her finger onto a scanner, going in when the final lock clicked open. The air inside was refreshing, and the smell of *Karenpack* tea kept her sane. There were files and papers and folders fitted into every slot imaginable. She had only one thing set on her mind today. She needed to find a newspaper. A newspaper from 12 years ago. Because she knew something no one else did. She knew how Esta Raven had disappeared.

Chapter 7

She headed towards her bookshelves. Papers and articles for all sorts of people and happenings crowded the shelves, letting hardly any of her books breathe. She found the book she was looking for, an escapologist book, and held its spine, pushing it downwards. The bookshelf cried, as it slowly shuffled to the left, revealing a corridor behind. Erle smirked. It was an old party trick, an *escapologist* trick. She walked down, stopping at an invisible barricade. "Fear or be feared. You choose," she muttered. The barricade disappeared. Voice command. She entered a small room, filled with webs and dust. She couldn't remember the last time she had been here.

She breathed into the decayed, stale air, coughing on cue. The room was filled knee-deep with snippets of neglected newspapers and yellow letters from long-forgotten presidents, royals, and ministers. Erle screwed her nose at the thought of the Minister. He was a foul man, and constantly smelled of mildew and lemongrass. He appeared in so many galas, Erle gave up counting. He was the second most important figure to the Hegal and Wyrmine. He organised all the banishments and exile. He also happened to be the Athkarvas' greatest enemy. He scrounged Vasilioroi for any Athkarva who outran the Regal Soldiers. If he found out about the Dracoros, people who were chased lived a life of hide and seek. People like her.

Erle shifted through stacks of worn-out papers until she found it. She saw what she was looking for. The newspaper article that was printed out 12 years ago.

Citizens of Silverpeak

A disappearance and planned leave aren't so different at all. Two weeks ago, Our Royal Majesty Hergal and Our Royal Highness Wyrmine's daughter and heir to the throne of Silverpeak and surrounding Counties, Princess Estella Raven was deemed an Athkarva. The ritual took place exactly a week before the November Feast, and a few days after the princess's 15th birthday. Several meetings and conferences confirmed Estella will NOT be the heir to the throne and her place will be taken by her younger sister, Aurella Raven, who is currently of age 13. Estella was to be taken away to the Royal Camp, where she was to stay until she had passed. She would not have received the same treatment as Common folk. But it is with great melancholy that it has come to know that Estella has escaped, on the day of the feast. Reporters assume that key reasons may include the fact she would not be heir, is an Athkarva, and being banished. More reports will be coming soon. There will also be extensive searches for our unusual princess, whom many now call a BLOOD TRAITOR. But many suspect the former heir planned her departure, which was not an accident. If this theory is true, we will hopefully find out. Gratcha to the Royal Office and Palace.

Gratcha.

A word she heard so often but never once to her. A sending of consolations she had never received, but had heard a time so many times. Estella Raven's *disappearance* left the capital in shambles, scrambling for a balance. Every country, every city needed a powerful figure—especially the Capital. Erle was from the capital, and she had seen the annual ritual for years until it was finally hers. She was born to two Kolospus, making her chances of being one even brighter than ever. But her chances failed her, just like everyone else. She was an Athkarva. And so was Estella.

It was unheard of, to be an Athkarva when both of your parents were Kolospi. Their blood combined resulted in it. But Erle was, and no one understood why. There had only been one other person like that. Estella.

People were stupid, and stupid people did stupid things. And many people were like that. Assumptions and speculations about her gathered around like a mighty, strong wind, pressuring her into hiding. People thought she was the Lost Queen. They consumed her, drowning her in their ignorant minds.

But she knew. She knew where Estella had gone- and why. She had been suspecting it for years, *3 years*. Her hesitation to confirm her findings slowed her down. But her constant procrastinating had its consequences. She only had 24 days. And time was running out. She pulled out another article. This one had been handled more recently, for the lack of dust on it assured her of it. She had highlighted the sentence that intrigued her most.

'Aurela was not present at the November feast'

Erle smirked. Bingo. Erle had been determined to find out what happened to her apparent bloodsake. Five years ago, was Erle's ritual day. She was in the front aisle, anxiously waiting for her turn. It came. Then she was banished. She was sent to the coast of Silverpeak, a good 6 hours away from the capital. Where all the impure lived, in striking poverty, other Athkarvas lined up next to her, staring at her in awe. Erle stayed silent, looking away from the burning gaze. She missed her parents, who begged the Hergal to spare her. But he was cold-hearted now, having lost his heir to the throne only a few several years ago. She had grown into a wealthy family, an influential family. She would have liked to stay in it.

But many things were unpredictable, such as a soul's fortune. Their fate. It was on that day Erle had learnt.

Nothing stays the same forever, except lost hope.

It was an art. Gripping on things should've deceased ages ago. Your skilled, crafty fingers grabbing hold of something even when you know it won't work. It was the faint glimmer of hope that kept you going. But when that's lost, *game over*.

Just because you were born into it, doesn't mean you'll die with it.

But it also doesn't mean you won't be able to retrieve it. And that's what gave Erle hope.

A ship.

There was a ship as well.

Its roar as it cut through the Archideon sea, almost as loud as the great thumping in her overworked heart. They were going to take her away.

But Erle managed to escape. She was an exception. A special case. She had friends who helped her escape. Friends with powers so strong, they could destroy *kingdoms* with a snap of a finger.

She has been in the deptarment of the Dracoros since. She was meant to join them, 5 years ago. Instead, she ran away and hid in woods, abandoned towers of failed Hergals, and underground bunkers from previous military movements. But they always managed to find her. Always.

They knew everything about her, and how much she knew about the princess who disappeared from her rightful throne 7 years ago. And it gave them the most excellent satisfaction to attack, vomit out the truth from her adamant body. Why? For the reward money of course. The council and the Royals started campaigns to find their daughter again, giving out a large sum of money to whoever found her or knew of her whereabouts. Eventually, she joined. Pressured by the constant threats that came her way.

Erle breathed softly, laughing quietly to herself. Relief. Her mind drifted off to a distant memory, she was right, and she had always been. She knew something no one else did. And that sort of power was dangerous.

Estella was a mistake, a malfunction. And Aurella has something to do with it.

Chapter 8

I was there. I was there the day, the hour, and *the moment* my sister disappeared. And it's all my fault. It was a flaw. A flaw in the system. An error. I had asked. I asked *them*. The people who convinced my vulnerable sister to change who she was forever. Manipulated her, manipulated her mind, manipulated her *blood*. And I tried, so hard, to get her away from them. 12 years have gone by, and so many things have changed, but there's one thing that hasn't.

If you can't beat 'em, join 'em

Chapter 9

It was time. Time to finally, *finally* understand why she was like this. All these years, Erle was scared. But not anymore. Not when there are hardly 24 days left before, she officially ruins her life, and believe me she has come concerningly close. She needs to find out why she's like this. Every other person who said this to her died, not living up to their own words. But it's now or never.

Chapter 10

Kai adjusted herself in the cell, turning around uncomfortably, trying to make a mental list of all the things that had happened to her in the past 2 hours.

-She met up with her now ex-colleague preparing to inform her of the change of departments when she came to know he has a secret basement filled with pictures of missing people and needs to find the princess.

-She *willingly* got kidnapped by a minor ready to throw his life away.

-She met the person who she believed killed her parents and learnt about a top-secret revolution.

-She is now stuck in a cell without air conditioning feeling sad.

Her list made her cringe. What on earth was she doing here? She was a detective, an insecure, *Mierchir* Coast detective. She had to come up with a plan, and she needed to do it now.

There is no plan. It was just clocking past 12. Kai closed her eyes, tucked her hair behind her ears and sighed. She was ready. She clicked her fingers and her whole body transformed. She didn't look different. In fact, you couldn't even see her. There was a reason she was taken in by Mierchir Coast. She was a great asset. Her power was simple but dangerous. And what was that power, you may ask? Just invisibility.

But not only was she invisible. Everything she touched became invisible until she returned to her original state.

She fingered her pocket and pulled out a bobby pin. A good detective always had a bobby pin, not for fashion. She didn't need to do espionage in style. She knew she already looked great. Look at her go. Her insecurities were already deteriorating. Kai smirked. No one would see her anyway. She secured the bobby pin inside the lock. After a few tries, she heard a satisfying click. No one was around. This society was so underfunded they couldn't even afford a security guard.

She still didn't have a well-formed idea of what she would be doing now. She assessed where she was now. Leaving her cell behind her, her sharp eyes began to collect every detail.

Next to her cell was its number. *24.* She speculated she was on a lower floor, the large metal set of stairs leading up to another level. The air was murky and unclean, cobwebs grouped in corners. A singular light bulb hung from the ceiling, letting out the dimmest of light. Several cells were situated alongside hers, each abandoned and unoccupied but just as filthy as hers. There was a camera positioned near the steps, glaring at her, with its gleaming lens, clean of cobwebs. Someone had been here.

She swiftly closed the cell's rusted door, her heart skipping every other beat—finally, time for the action.

Chapter 11

Kai stood over her laptop, debating whether she should really be typing such personal matters on a work screen. *Screw it*. She's lived here for 3 years, she's going to mould her own rights. She clicked the keys, the sound of them ticking away ringing in her ears. She hovered over the search bar, contemplating. Making her own decisions felt unfamiliar, others gripping on strings tied tightly across her shoulder, like puppets. Controlling her every move. But she had broken free. What had urged her? She had no idea. Perhaps the Coast worker, maybe the revolution, maybe her own conscience. But it was time. Her fingers poked the keys. She pulls up an article. Released just a few Eras ago. Something she had not been able to see, its presence absent in her obsessive shrine of newspaper, and her ruling fear limiting her knowledge. She was breaking the Code and Conduct Of The ARA. Its words clearly state the restriction of awareness of one's past life via other persons and modern technology. Translating that her past was only to be remembered through her conscience.

19 Sacred Era

Her Sacred Princess Aurella Ismene Raven has now gone missing. 8 Sacred Era ago, Ex Sacred Princess Estella Amabel Raven vanished from her imprisonment after her blood proved to be marked. Aurella went missing exactly 8 Eras later, the night before the feast and a week before Estella's birthday. There has been only one suggestion regarding her disappearance, one many believe to be set by herself. A note, reading "A clone, I seek her destroyer and her creator, all who is her clone." Forces have been called from all over the globe to testify to this lone piece of evidence that may provide any piece of information to guide the Royals of her location. Tension is slowly but steadily making its way along Silverpeak as the new heir to throne is now indefinite and questions have been raised. More answers will be coming soon— Gratcha to The Royal Head Family and the Council.

"A clone" A memory clocked inside her mind as if someone had dusted the cobwebs away, and she recognised it. During the duration of her hiding, news about assumptions about the clone was uncovered as it had been several years since either of the sisters was found. Many people supposed the princess was dead, her task of finding the clone failing. But she had a different theory. A theory she knew was correct.

She was the clone.

Her parents never gave her much insight into her life. She didn't look like her parents. Her ma's hair was gleaming silver with speckles of metallic blue. Her pa's ginger mane. But hers? A simple black, contrasting her pale face. People told her that she wasn't born into this family. But could she have been an experiment? An experiment gone wrong?

She could distinctly remember crouching on the grand staircases in her parents' house, listening to them argue about her. What if she was modified? It was a curious thought And, it unsettled her. So as any logical person would do, she decided to wait until 1 in the morning (the time she trusted to be the most holy) and go after her thoughts until caught up to them. A ping came up on her monitor, it was Noah. He was one of Juniper's most trusted allies in the Time of Troubles.

His brother worked in the Council, as one of the Special 12. People who made the most valuable decisions. Noah didn't have to join the Dracoros. But he did anyway, learning about it from his brother. He worked as a spy.

She clicked on the message. Oh no. The Coast member she had seen earlier this evening had escaped. Honestly, she found this funny. She found it funny how a bunch of excluded people inside an abandoned underground *base* thought they could go against a fully trained Coast member. But she remembered the Dracoros were not to be sold short. It wasn't just this branch. Nearly 50 different outlets were scattered across the country. Each one housing over a thousand Athkarvas and curious oddities.

She could hear the sirens now, blaring through the speakers, the sound was so loud she could feel it inside her very bones. Erle got up and put on her hood. Safety precaution. She went out the way she came in, passing by Edwin's lab. The room remained shut. She saw her colleagues peering out of their secret rooms, trying to figure out why the alarm was ringing. Only a handful of people would have received the message from Noah. 1 or 2 detectives, Erle (because she worked in research, it gave her a well-rounded view of people and their motives) and a few bodyguards. She saw Noah anxiously huddled up near Juniper, his face lacking colour. "I locked her up. In Cell 24, floor -2, with a camera right opposite. I even left Cairo in there. To make sure she wasn't getting into any trouble. We need her for the experiment. And the information." he blubbered. Juniper showed no expression, her eyebrows just slightly creasing, reading her emotions was always close to impossible. But from what Erle could infer, Noah had let her down, for the first time. Juniper raised her head, her eyes looking straight at her. 5 other people lined up against her, only 2 of whom she knew the name of. First, there was Everest, a detective. He was incredibly mysterious, hardly ever tolerating discussion. It was what, she supposed, made him a good detective. He was focused on his job. No distractions. He had a twin, Leila. Erle had seen her a few times. But she wasn't here today. There was also Leigh, a bodyguard. She wasn't a bodyguard for her physical strength. It was her magic. So powerful it could make the toughest people come down to her knees and beg for mercy. She wasn't an Athkarva. She was a necromancer. She whispered to souls that had been long forgotten, pulling them from the dirt and soil like ribbon, and sentencing them to live inside a person's head. Eating their way out. There were very few of her kind. All of them were sentenced to execution. But she escaped and found herself here.

Juniper took out a wine glass and smashed it to the ground, pieces of crystal lay on the hard ground. She waved the hand around until a picture of the Coast member appeared, made up of tiny shards of glass. She glared at the group and whispered hoarsely *"**Find her**"*

Chapter 12

Kai ran, with no sense of where she was going. Every side was a dead end. She could hear the alarm. They would be onto her anytime. It would be best if she found a place to hide until everything settled down. Then she would start her investigation.

She went up the set of stairs, more cells. But at the back of the floor, she could see a room, the door held ajar. She worked towards it cautiously. There were prisoners on this floor. One or two corpses were lying on the ground, their clothes being chewed away by hungry moths, and their skin slowly but surely shrivelling up.

She then heard a whisper, from someone who sounded extremely familiar. Her heart started thumping quicker than ever. She could feel her body tense up, nearly paralysed from shock. She turned her head around, her neck feeling more rusted than an antique clock.

Alok. He looked more worn out compared to this afternoon. His hair was messy, and his cloak was wrinkled and tattered. A fresh wound was marked across his forehead to his chin, blood still seeping out. Its colour was a midnight blue, clearly representing his culture. He smirked. Her eyebrows shot up. Questions flooded her brain, confusion washed over her face. She tumbled over her words, trying to frame a logical sentence. Alok put his hand up. "Get these damn handcuffs off me first". Kai then realised that he was still in his cell. She got out her bobby pin and unlocked the cell, then his handcuffs. He got up slowly, groaning. "I probably have chronic back pain now," he sighed. Kai opened her mouth, about to start questioning him. Alok cut her off, getting there first. "I saw that weird guy taking you, and I found it interesting. I needed a distraction from Estella anyway. So, I put on my special fun little shadow and followed him. And then he caught me. And now I'm here!" He said, smiling. His generally daunting expression had melted, contrasting with how she had seen him this afternoon. Kai pointed to his injury. "Well, obviously I fought. But we shouldn't be underestimating this lot, but I did kill the security guard." He stated calmly, eyeing the corpse lying beside his cell. She hadn't realised that earlier. Alok walked towards her. "Something is happening. I'm not sure what, but we got to find out. They thought I was knocked out, but I wasn't. They were talking about some revolution." She nodded. "The head of this place was responsible for the Council Attack a few Eras ago. She's still alive." Alok's eyebrows shot up, his mouth opening, about to say something else when they both heard heavy footsteps, thumping down the cold, metal stairs. Alok and Kai shared a look and ran in opposite directions. Kai hid inside one of the empty cells, hoping no one would find her or that the prisoners would tell. Her eyes were fixated on the room that she was about to go into before she saw Alok. The door was now completely closed. The air was still as if it were holding its breath.

She pulled out the dagger she hid inside her pocket, and tucked the strands of hair that blocked her eyes behind her ears. She started breathing slowly, trying to balance out her thoughts. The first person descended their footsteps softer than a rabbit. It was hard to see in the darkness, but Kai could tell it was a woman. She stopped suddenly, and looked up the stairs, bringing her hand up, her lips slowly mouthing the words "wait". She wasn't holding anything, and her face was hard to read. Her feet touched the ground, the soles of her boots clicking softly. She walked down the floor cautiously, looking at both sides before reaching the edge. Her eyes clicked into place staring. Staring right at her. Her face finally began to show expression. Her eyebrows jerked upwards, her eyes popping out. She recomposed herself, before looking back and firmly shaking her head. She went back upstairs. Kai had escaped.

Chapter 13

3 hours went by, and Erle sat on the edge of her cot, her palm perched on the cold, metal frame. The search had been conducted, to no avail. They had failed to find the Coast member, and precautionary mail had been sent to the people. Until they managed to find her, the Dracoros had to be extra careful. Juniper was furious, her face turning into the colour of a ripened tomato, her cheeks flushed in a vermillion red. Anger spread across her face, as Leigh told her the news. All the search members were put into isolation, including her. Which was ludicrous, ironic even. Erle had managed to see her, the Coast member. Her eyes met hers. She could feel a

connection, unlike anything she had felt ever before. The fear in the coast member's eyes sparked something inside her, but she wasn't sure what quite yet.

She opened her notebook, the little leather burgundy one, that she hid inside a small wooden crate, which stored all of her limited belongings. She pulled out the singular pen she had and flipped through the pages of her book, her eyes scanning all the bits of information she had written in it over the years. It was sort of like her memoir, narrating any particularly interesting events that had happened to her. It was given to her by a merchant, nearly 7 years ago. Back when she still lived a relatively ordinary life. She would often visit the town with her sister Mira, in secret. Her parents forbid her from mingling with the village lot, after her coming of age of 13. Which was hardly possible, seeing as her best friend Lili was a village girl. Mira liked going to the village market, which contained stalls with jewellery, clothes, food, and trinkets beyond measure. It was there that Erle had met the merchant. He was a man of travel, passionate about journeying the world. He was magic as well. Gifted in design, his fingertips are capable of art. He specially designed the notebook, its colour chosen after Erle's last name. *Bloodstone.* Its pages are lighter than feathers, and smoother than silk. He made her the pen as well, its cherry wood material and polished finish.

Her pen glided over the pages like water entering the cracks and creases of an eroding landscape. She wrote in it every day, but somehow it never ran out of pages, the book was larger than her face, stories of her life etched in its body. She flipped to a fresh page and started writing.

The revolution is on its way, but are we ready?

She stopped to think for a moment. Her ma had taught her breathing exercises before she had gone to the coast, a mere 30 minutes before the ship had come to take her away. It was the last time she had ever seen her ma.

She focused on her pulse, which always seemed to work. She breathed slowly, letting her worries slowly out with it. Her roommate-Eleanore lay fast asleep in her cot, snoring softly. It was 11 o'clock, and the quarters were dead silent. She lifted her pen to write another sentence when she heard a faint clicking noise. She stayed where she was, stiff and terrified. She reached into her pocket, fingering a retractable knife (another one of random memorabilia) and calculating the time her door would open. She always locked it, no matter what time of day it was. She even told her roommate to do it. Erle cautiously got up and proceeded towards the door, the clicking noise still prominent. It was easily recognisable as someone picking the lock, and just as she was about to do something, the door slammed open, pushing her away. She fell on her back, on the hard floor, her roommate jolted up, her eyes wide open in terror. The figures stood at the doorframe, one man and one woman. She immediately recalled the female to be the one she saw this evening and ignored. She wasn't sure why she did it, but she was ready to do it again. But the man brought no memories to her. He peered into the room, his eyebrows raising. He then put his hand out, signalling her to shake it. The woman stared at her, her head held high, but her messed up hair and dirt-covered face ruined the effect. She said one sentence that would change the course of her life forever.

"I know what you're looking for, and I'll help you find it"

Chapter 14

"Are you insane?" Alok yelled at her, his disbelief visible. Kai put up her hand, stopping him in his tracks. She was one of the few people who could resist his unpleasant personality. "It would help us too. I have eyes everywhere Alok, all over this building. I used the special little cameras the engineer made us. Well of course I take them everywhere. How else would I get that Dracorus on our side? No, I know she's an Athkarva, but I never liked that idea anyway y'know? It's not like we'll tell everyone about her. Shut your mouth, Alok, it's a good idea and you know it." They were hiding in a secret part of the vast underground building, Erle had taken them there, and she had gone back to get some files about Estella. Kai still had four of the cameras she had gotten from the engineer back in Mierchir Coast. The engineer was magic, a good magician not like the ones who were banished. He enchanted them to travel to their wanted place by the whisper of their keeper, and they could follow the most discrete and generic commands as well. Kai simply had to say "Go to the places with the most information" and they just led their own path. She could monitor them and look through their lens using a USB stick connected to her laptop, which could make itself fit in a pocket with a single button, also made by the engineer. Kai made a mental note to appreciate him when she got back.

Erle arrived, her arms full of papers and documents. She was out of breath as well. But surprisingly so, I was not in the slightest scared. Coast members were Athkarvas biggest fears, their whole reason for banishment. She was faced with one right now, and from what Kai could tell, she hadn't even broken into a sweat. She seemed a bit tired, that's all, which was understandable. Living in an underground building for over 3 years, without seeing the light of day. Surely tired was the bare minimum you could say to expect.

Erle began her lengthy tale, and she was very thorough with it, trusting them like her own kin. Kai felt like she could understand her, though Alok seemed rather bored quite quickly. There was a revolution on the horizon, where Ahkarvas fought for their rights back. Personally, she agreed with this. Even Alok nodded his head, but neither of them would have dared to speak out about this. Kai had read every newspaper about Estella and the royal family. Waiting for some magnificent idea to come into her head and spark the breakthrough of her career. But she realised it was more than that to Erle. It was her entire life, and she spent hours every day obsessing over it, wondering if the princess was her clone and whether Aurella had something to do with it. For the first time in a very long time, Kai had a mystery that she needed to solve that wasn't just for the sake of her salary but for the welfare of someone. Even if that someone was an Athkarva she had meant hardly 4 hours ago who had saved her life, and of course Alok's too.

The 3 of them pieced together the information they could find about her disappearance and the whereabouts of Aurella. It surprised Kai just how much information someone had after being given near to no knowledge of the outside world compared to a committee of over 300 people to find 1 person, with more details about Esta than Esta herself.

Kai checked her watch, it was past 1 now. How long had they been here? Erle noticed her, and her face turned pale, imitating white, cold marble. Her facial features became stiff and rigid. She blinked forcefully, looking left and right to make sure no one was coming. "There's extra security after they found out you escaped," she said looking at Kai. Alok was half asleep, it was obvious he wanted to go home, his hands were in his pockets, fingering a pocket knife. Instinct. *"Expect the unexpected"* was the first thing you would learn when you started training.

"You ok," Kai asks, concerned. Erle slowly whispers "It's 1, the guards will be still on their shifts, and this is the first general area they patrol, our whispers mustn't be heard, or there's no way any of us will get out here alive." Kai nods her head and gently nudges Alok, smirking. He gets up with a start, murmuring. The three get up, and Erle leads the way down to her office. No had been here apart from her, and she found this awfully unnatural.

She turned around to face Kai, who stared at her blatantly and back at the room. She smiled to herself softly. "You can sleep here, just make sure no one sees you," Erle says. Alok and Kai lay on the floor, before chatting with her for a while longer.

Chapter 15

It was a long trek to Weardili, and I was already starting to get tired. But my heart kept at it, trying its hardest to support me and Esta. I had lied to myself, saying that Estella wasn't a victim, but she had fallen into the trap like many others. People who risked everything, even their blood, *their soul*, for protection. Most Kolupsi lived a safe life, away from danger or risk, but not my sister. Oh no. She was threatened, from all corners, to confess. Confess the sins she had been committing. Sins I will soon find out. That was her reason to change. I refused to believe anything else that anyone would try to tell me. I shan't give up. I had everything I needed, served to be on a golden platter, and now was the time to use it.

I looked at the map I had drawn for years, gathering every little piece of information I could.

I was already a quarter way through, and everything was going smoothly. Something wrong was bound to happen. There was a shortcut to my destination, reducing my travel journey by almost 3x-but it was also the riskiest. When I met the guide, he warned me of the route. It was the underground path, where the Dracoros HQ is located. I remembered the person I magicked into giving me the information, and I wondered how he was doing now.

I contemplated on what I should do for a good 5 minutes, as I had put this off since the beginning of the journey. Finally, I came to a decision. I shall go down the underground path that started from *Igmore River*, went right across the HQ and straight into the Military camp. Which is where I knew my *'beloved'* sister resided. It all clicked together, like pieces in a puzzle. 2 years after Esta's disappearance, the Time of Troubles began, also when several sightings of her formed. Father didn't believe any of them. He sent all the men who came up with that sort of theory to death, just like the cold-hearted bloodthirsty man he had become. Her fingerprints lay across the weapons and staff that the Coast had found, proving she wasn't dead. A high level of weapon trading happened in the Weardili area. The same weapons that contained her fingerprints. Coincidence? I think not.

I began the treacherous trek to Igmore River, found nearly 30 miles away. My body started to ache all over, and carrying my food basket was a constant chore. This was a present from the magician, who I had bribed with 20 gold coins, to give me a magic basket, which created a supply of over 3x the contents inside of it, meaning if I put 2 apples inside, I would be gifted with 6 in hardly a second. But the catch? It was heavier than brick, weighing me down even further, along with my bag and general exhaustion. My bottle had the same enchantment, with the same catch. I sipped on my water greedily, taking it in like fine, silky honey. I was starting to feel faint, but after 2 days (which felt like a week since I wasn't the most athletically able person) I arrived at the river. I sat down at the edge and dipped my feet inside. The Dracoros told me that entering the path was a tricky process. It required jumping in, finding a golden pebble, knocking it twice, and clicking your fingers. I laughed at this. It sounded more like a cliche fairytale than a most wanted society Military base. It surprised me how a community with no funds or money could have such an influence on so many people, and have a military base stronger than the Country's.

I dived into the river, my luggage's weight made me gasp, my mouth wide open in shock. I gulped in a large amount of water, as I wailed my arms about, nearly forgetting how to swim. My lungs filled with water, restricting me from breathing. I couldn't come back up either. My bags were bullying me down. My heart started beating faster than it had ever before, and blood rushed to my heart. I turned my head this way and that, until I finally spotted a lone golden pebble, I swam towards it as quickly as possible, and knocked on it twice. As I clicked my fingers, a large hole appeared in front of me, the pebbles and coral disappearing, replaced by a big circle of nothingness. I jumped in and found myself hitting my head hard on the mud. I felt around me and breathed a sigh of relief. I was in the tunnel, and I was alive.

Chapter 16

It had been 2 days. Erle had been checking up on the Coast members every 4 hours, tending to them like newborn babies. Both Kai and Erle had formed quite a connection, their difference in blood not stopping their relationship. They were pretty much on the same side. The side of innocence, and peace. Just for two different causes. Kai could see that Alok felt quite left out, which was unusual for him, wavering his reputation as a tough, unpleasant man who was not to be crossed.

Plans were in the making, and ideas were shared. None of the contributions came from Alok. It was getting on Kai's nerves now. His ego stretched further than the fields in the south. The revolution was now 22 days away, and Erle was getting more and more perturbed, and full of nerves. Alarms had been placed around the entire building, under the courtesy of Edwin. Erle and he had worked quite closely over the 2 days, jotting out a plan to execute the mechanical part of the revolution. Such as any gadgets for communication and networking. Edwin was the hands and Erle was the brain, and they worked tightly together. It hurt her to keep secrets from him, but it had to be done.

Every time she checked on Kai and Alok, she had a little bit more information on the revolution. Together, they mapped out a detailed scheme to cover all their group objectives. Find Estella, end the revolution before it even started, and (try) to stop the discrimination and treatment of Athkarvas. Alok shook his head at this proposal, stating the impracticality of completing these tasks before the deadline- 22 days. At last, the girls convinced him, the clock ticking to twilight. Now, just 21 days. They would start their trip at midnight tomorrow, going in the route to the Military Base, seeing as Erle had a pass to go to all Dracoras camps, bases and hideouts. It would be quite tricky to get both Alok and Kai through the security checks spread across the path, but it won't be impossible. Erle hadn't gone to sleep for over 3 days, her mind focused on the location of her 'clone' and the ticking of the clock for the revolution. She was feeling more antsy than ever.

The entire day droned on, Edwin and she worked on an eye that could detect people in a 2-mile radius. Erle wasn't entirely sure how she would cover her disappearance, but she hoped that it wouldn't matter in the end, maybe the Coast would grant her the gift to live a normal life, not hiding underground and making machines for genocide. Every spare minute she got, she looked through her special notebook, for anything useful for their journey. She knew where Esta was, she was on a Military Base. It was quite obvious, and it surprised her that nobody else had thought of it. She wasn't sure how it was obvious either, but it just was, it emerged in her mind like magic.

Finally, the witching hour arose. She met up with the 2, who were already ready. They were wearing the same clothes as she had first seen them, understandable considering they hadn't been home in over 3 days. Erle brought out the trunk she stored, with all of her belongings she had brought from her room last night. It was also filled with files and papers for clues as to where Esta had gone. Alok seemed to be in a better mood today, and he listened to the brush through of their plan. The first stop would be the Ignore River, exactly 45 miles away. Alok had arranged for a car to take them there, from one of his good friends, Astor. Erle used one of Edwin's techs to communicate with him. It will be here in about 15 minutes. The trip to the river would take around an hour due to the several precautions that will be taken to ensure the secrecy of their travel.

Of course, she brought her handsome notebook, along with the files, some impressive bits of tech that would prove to be of the utmost useful. Time was ticking away, and it filled Erle with worry. It was also a shock when Alok produced a staff he had been hiding for the past few days, it even surprised Kai.

"What? You thought I was just gonna waltz into a criminal mastermind's private asylum by following a hooded man, taking away my colleague without the slightest bit of protection? Idiot." He said smugly, smirking. She could see the hurt on Kai's face when this was said, but with the quick dismissal of it, Erle was about to ask if she was ok, when the communication gadget beeped quietly.

It was time

Chapter 17

The car was far simpler than Erle had imagined. But it was fair enough, seeing as they needed to blend in with the normal people as much as possible. There was a security vault in the back, disguised as the boot, with a passcode lock and everything. This was the first time Erle had been in a car in a long time, and it felt good. It created the fake euphoria that rushed through her veins and the adrenaline flooded her mind, at the thought of doing something good in the world, something that will satisfy both divisions of the world. A chance- something she had never been given. A chance to prove herself was all she needed. And that went for all of them.

After an hour of lounging in the car, anxiously waiting for their destination, they arrived. The air was clearer, less heavy, and it felt like honey in Erle's lungs, after years underground. It was like drinking fresh, precious water in a desert after strolling in sandy dunes for days. Erle welcomed it wholeheartedly. Alok stared at the river in wonder, taking in the view. "This place is even better in real life, compared to the pictures." He whispered. Both Alok and Kai stared at her expectantly. Erle realised she was the only one who knew how to get through the river into the tunnel.

After all three of them jumped through the hole, and after they had recovered from the fall, they discussed the plan. It would take many days to reach the military base, and along the way, there would be 4 security checks, to verify that there wouldn't be any spies to copy them or rat on them. Erle let her fingertips glide over the smooth surface of her access card. There were many risks embedded in the process of getting to the base, and many were extremely obvious as well. Firstly, Juniper may have figured out what was going on before the group had reached any of the security checks and deactivated her card. Both Kai and Alok could also get caught, which would raise even more suspicion, and all theories would lead to her saying that she had found and helped the Coast members to escape, this was one of the greatest offences you could commit as a member of Dracoras. This would easily result in all three of them being publicly tortured and executed in the Military Base itself, seeing as that was where they contained most of their weapons. It would take at least a week to journey through the tunnel, to reach the first security check, and their food supply was hardly generous.

Erle had snuck into the food lab of the building last night, managing to gather an odd collection of food and supplies. She had also managed to get to the canteen, through the kitchens, where robots cooked and cleaned impersonating a human. She needed an access card to get through, which she stole from one of the robots, which were charging up at the back, doing it so quickly there wasn't enough time to raise an alarm. She found sacks full of produce and freezers with meat and dairy. She filled her basket, which was ever so small but could carry an endless supply. She was at this for over 2 hours, silently praying no one was awake at this ungodly hour. But she still doubted this was enough. It was a leap of fate when there was nothing more than an abyss of peril and danger.

They had only walked 5 hours with approximately 18 pit stops for a break before the lot was ravenous.

They left the HQ on an empty stomach, even though Kai munched on an energy bar on the way to the river. It was incredible to hear how the tunnel was completely dry, despite the river that was right above it, and the fact that the water didn't flow through the cavity in the river into the tunnel. But the ground was bumpy and uneven, making it harder to walk across. It tired them quicker, until finally, all the energy left their body. Erle pulled out the basket. The three of them had turns to carry the basket, so they wouldn't lose any more energy than necessary. She lifted the lid, and the smell of aged bread and slowly decaying produce hit her, nearly making her eyes water. She brought out some near-expired strawberry jam and spread it across 3 slices of bread. The complex carbs and sugar should keep them going for another several hours. She handed the slices out to the others, who were sitting against the tunnel, exhausted and panting. The build-up of lactic acid intoxicates their bodies, disabling them from the slightest movement of their legs without a subtle groan. Erle was used to this, the constant running and tiredness. She wasn't entirely sure whether that was a good or bad thing. But there were more important things she could be thinking about while munching on her crumbling bread and jam. The sweetness hurt her gums and she could feel cavities producing in her teeth. She was lucky to never have had a cavity in her life. *Lucky.*

Chapter 18

I felt lightheaded. And my legs were giving way. It felt like the tunnel walls were getting closer, trapping me in a cage. Like a rabid animal. Maybe I was going crazy. Maybe spending days in a constricting tunnel did that to someone. Every part of me was aching. I was starting to trip over myself, almost drunk. I remembered my safety coach teaching me ways to deal with different situations. After Esta disappeared, conspiracies of her being kidnapped were consistent. Fearing the new heir would be kidnapped, they hired 7 bodyguards to protect me and a safety coach. He told me that when I was feeling dizzy, sugar was the quickest route out. I opened up my casket and gagged. I had been eating the same 3 things for the past 4 days for every meal-Brie, crackers and grenchita. The grenchita was my personal favourite, but after the constant taste of its bitter juice and sugary outer shell, the mere sight of it was enough for my stomach to start churning. I picked it up now, the sugary coating rubbing off on my fingertips, I held it towards my mouth. The familiar sense of nauseousness returned. I bit into it, the overwhelming bitterness and sweetness flooding my mouth like an unwelcome wave. At last, my legs surrendered, and I fell onto the ground, hard. I started to get a migraine. But after a few deep breaths, it went away. My dizziness disappeared but my heart started thumping out of my chest, faster than I thought possible. I pressed the tips of my fingers with my thumb, skipping the middle. A calming technique my ma had taught me when I was still small, and ignorant. When I was scared of little things like insects I found in the Royal Garden, or the moving creatures on my plate- supposedly a family recipe passed down generations of royal blood. When my father had to go to war, and on the day of my ceremony. The walls were still closing in on me, consuming me and whispering in my ear. The overwhelming and debilitating fear made its way around my entire body. What was going on? I could feel the sweat forming on my forehead. Was this a panic attack?

I had never had one before. Or perhaps claustrophobia? The dizziness came back, and I dropped the grenchitha. My feet felt numb, the painful sensation of pins and needles persisting. I looked around, taking in the scene, a grenchitha with one bite taken out of it, her casket with its lid still open, and some red dye on the ground. My eyes flickered, almost like a cassette, as I took in what I just saw. That red dye looked a lot like blood. That's when I noticed the lingering stinging on my knee. I gasped, then cringed at the pain it caused. It must have happened when I fell, my dizziness, a creature with its mind. My jeans were ripped where that nasty gash was located. Pink flesh and crimson blood made me nearly heave. I was also not aware I could have a fear of blood. I had learnt many things today. One other thing I learned was that I would not be able to stand up or continue to walk. I was helpless. My carefully thought-out plan that had been on-going for more than 3 years had come to an end in less than a week. It broke my heart. I ripped it into the same could be said for my jeans—all that hard work for nothing. I wondered if Ma and Pa knew I was gone yet. Who am I kidding? They probably didn't care. Ma had depression, she sat alone in her chamber for hours on end. Only answering calls from me or a glass or two (or 4) of red wine. Pa was never even home. Out in war. Fighting battles that he knew he wouldn't win. I didn't know why I was thinking about them, I tended to focus my mind on more practical things. I had more important things I needed to focus on. If I wanted to move in the next few hours, I needed to get my leg cleaned up. I looked through my bag to find my emergency kit. I produced a couple of rolls of bandages and saline solution along with a few other things. I wasn't a trained professional but this was fairly straight forward, wasn't it? I carefully cleaned up the wound using some alcohol wipes. I winced at the sharp pain, dabbing away at the blood while trying to breathe steadily. It wasn't as bad as my other injuries, from my unceasing fencing, and sword fighting lessons. The minimal pain was owed to the nurses who never faltered in sending me to the sick chamber and smearing my wounds and gashes with herbal ointment which stings for a minute but then relieves me from all the pain. I yearn for that now, regretting my foolishness to fail to bring it along with me. I stay put on the ground and close my eyes. I wish that time would reverse, I wouldn't have to look for Esta, because she would have never left. She would never have been lured into changing who she was, our family wouldn't have broken. And I wouldn't have needed to cry all those nights away when instead I could be talking to my big sister. That's all I needed. Just my big sister. I dozed off.

Chapter 19

Erle pulled out her watch, it had been just over 24 hours since they had begun. The mud walls merged, turning into a tan gloop. Kai had a piercing headache, howling as she stumbled over the bumps and rocks. Alok was silent, not participating in conversations, and not eating much food. Kai guessed this was his ego acting up. He was starting to look a little bit pale as well, all colour draining from his face. The straight tunnel now had split into 2 or 3 several times, and the group had to guess where to go. There was no easy way out. They were taking breaks more often now, but still making good progress. It would only take them another

4-5 days until they reached the Base Camp, and they were just a few dozen miles away from reaching their first security checkpoint. However, Erle didn't want to disturb the peaceful quiet, a rare treat for her, the groaning of prisoners in the basements and Juniper and her circle of higher position members barking orders. Especially in planning for the revolution. But the peace wouldn't last for long. They still hadn't managed to fabricate a convincing tale for their visit to the security check, and it was now at her utmost priority, she would bring it up tonight, after their final 2 hours before some well-needed sleep. They walked on for another hour until they saw another split direction. Erle looked at the others, raising her eyebrows. Alok pointed left, Kai pointed right, and they both stared at her. It was her deciding vote. Alok looked dreadful, it was surprising what just 24 hours could do to you. It was almost as if this place were enchanted. Or perhaps cursed? It didn't matter right now. Erle thought it would do him some good for them to do something in his favour. She pointed left, and that's where they headed. It was difficult without a map, but they had to make do with Erle's limited knowledge from her coaching lessons when she first got recruited. The tunnel went on for ages, and it was unclear when it would stop. They weren't sure how long they'd been going, how long there was left. Hours merged by, passing by in seconds. Minutes for longer, strolling on and on. Erle's legs ached, to her embarrassment, thinking she was the toughest in the group. Alok was hardly up, drifting between states of being awake and dozing off. It appeared that Kai was the most active of the lot, though she possessed hardly any energy.

They had been planning a scheme to trick the security. Erle knew just how tight the provision was. Chances of managing to ploy were low, but it had to be done. Erle had been able to sneak into the lab, and brought along a few ingredients with her, encased in glass bottles. It was their only hope that the glass hadn't managed to shatter. She had also brought along the ingredients to make an invisibility potion. It was doubtful there'd be enough for Kai and Alok but they had no other ideas. The potion itself contained a few simple ingredients, but the process of combining them was meticulous. Erle's least favourite thing to do was make potions. It sounded like they were in a world where magic and supernaturals were praised, but this was not the case. They lived in a world of corruption and despair. Basic human needs were hard to obtain. She was starting to think about Juniper. What was going to happen? It was very likely that she had already figured out she had escaped. They could have alerted the security of the checkpoints already. This was not the time to think negatively. It would poison their bodies. But the thought lingered in Kai's head. The chances of their plan failing when she had prepared for this moment for 3 years. It was terrifying. Erle pulled out some ingredients. Snakeskin and frog skeletons are some of the few. She crushed the ingredients in a mortar and pestle set she had borrowed from Aarushi, her room neighbour. It wasn't exactly borrowing but more stealing. But Erle learnt to look past that. She kept the powdered mixture in another glass jar. The last ingredient was wet mud. Mud was all around them. They just needed water. After walking for a little longer, they saw a silhouette of a person, outlined in black and left as a little heap on the side of the wall. High point of the figure with fear in her eyes, her pupils dilated. They jogged towards the body. It was a female. Alok noticed her arms had gone limp, and the gauze wound up around her knee. It looked like she had been knocked out cold for hours. She wore dark blue jeans, stained with blood, a dark tank top, and heavy black boots. A gun and a sharpened knife were in her pocket, her palm placed above it. Her hair was a peachy blonde, tied up in a messy bun. She looked like she hadn't slept in days, the dark circles underneath her eyes a trace of her trauma. She almost looked peaceful, like she was resting. But no one could be peaceful with a leg injured like that. It was badly wrapped and dark red splotches were already appearing. Her chest was moving up and down softly, proving she was still alive, just unconscious. They didn't know how long she had been here. She didn't look too thin, so it hadn't been very long since she ate. She did look strong, with arms that looked like they would carry heavy loads, and legs that looked like they could walk miles without breaking. But who was she? Kai's eyebrows raised in realisation. Aurela-the royal princess- hadn't been seen publicly in over 6 years, due to her training. Her soft features had gone now, replaced by sharp lines. The smile lines were non-existent. Her hair had become darker, and her face lacked all the signs of childhood. She was still as beautiful as people remembered. Aurela hadn't been at the palace for over 5 Eras. What she had been doing out there was a mystery. They started debating whether they should leave her here or not., but settled on waking her up. It was a risky choice, considering they were acquaintances of a member of the most criminally active group in the country. And they were waking up the 3rd highest-ranking citizen in the country - the princess. But it wasn't too much of a problem. The princess was a fugitive on the run. *She was said to have a pretty face but a very ugly heart.* They weren't sure why, but maybe they were soon to find out.

Chapter 20

I was woken up by an unwelcome splash of water spraying across my face. I scrambled up and fell back down after my body comprehended the still-healing (not even started) gash on my knee. I noticed the smears of blood on the gauze, and cringed at my terrible job at first aid. My mind was still in a haze, like when you rub your eyes and see colours you had never seen before, the fogginess that enters your mind that acts as a shelter around confusion. Water trickled down my cheek, like tears. It brought back my sense of consciousness. Someone had found me. Whoever it was, I was going to be ok. The gun and knife were still safe in my jeans pocket, I could feel it, and it reassured me. My eyes, still blurry, adjusted over the lines and curves of three figures. They loomed near me. 2 females and one male. All 3 of them were rough, but nothing I couldn't handle. One of the females had silvery-blue hair, like a pixie. But that was stupid, pixies didn't exist. My mind was wandering again. My head-ached, I couldn't think straight. I focused on the man. He had jet-black hair and an edged jaw. His eyes drooped slightly, and he wore a silver stud on both ears and a snake on his right. He held out his hand, and I took it. Support would be most helpful and well appreciated. The girl with the silver hair wrapped her arm around my shoulder, stabilizing my body. A look of concern was on the other lady's face. I could've sworn I had seen her before, but I couldn't place my finger on it. "Hello, Your Highness" The 'other lady' said. I hadn't heard someone address me like that in years. It was unfamiliar. I whispered, "Aura, call me Aura." They most definitely knew who I was, even though they hadn't seen me in a while. Perhaps I was still recognisable. I hadn't looked at my reflection in 5 months. I was scared about what I would see. That's when I recognised who the lady was. *Kairinai.* An old detective set on the case to find my blood traitor of a sister and failed. I pitied her, she was probably the few people who had known me professionally. I knew who the man was as well. The only *Athkarva* not sentenced to the island. His capabilities proved useful. His name was Alok. I remember his cowardly brother, rumours spreading his disappearance having to do with this man of violence. He had also worked on the case about my sister, and he had of course failed. It tarnished the reputation of all the detectives, journalists, and Coast Members assigned to the case. Deeming them unqualified and inefficient with resources. Maybe that's why they chose to lead a life of crime. They had no choice. My sister had a choice. She could have just sat back, let father rule the country, and waited until it was her turn. Be quiet about things. That's what got her first in trouble. Her ability to be trusted. To keep secrets. She lacked that. So, she went the wrong way. And now, I have no choice but to follow her but try my very best to make the most minimal amount of mistakes along the way. I haven't done very well so far. The girl, the girl with silvery hair, had a badge on the left-hand side of her robe. A Times New Roman 'D' with a dragon layered on top. The logo was so familiar it made me gasp. It was the symbol of the group community she had been longing to see for so long. The exhilaration took her aback.

Kai must have seen the intoxicating happiness on my face. I lunged towards Erle and hugged her. I'm not sure why. I pointed at the badge and asked "Are you a member of Dracoros?" Fear flashed in her eyes, which wasn't too surprising. She was part of the most criminally active society in the country and she was talking to the princess. She looked like she was about to knock me out cold again when she slowly, and hesitantly nodded her head. I sighed, my blood full of serotonin, a kind of excitement I hadn't felt in years. The very first time, I was meeting a Dracorus who was against their type of work. I would get exclusive inside information. I started asking questions excitedly. The girl, who I now know as Erle- pointed her finger up. They asked questions first. It seemed like I could trust them. If I was wrong, I could've just made my first fatal mistake.

I told them. I told them everything. They were the very first people to have ever believed me and believed in my theories. They weren't theories any more. They were facts, and I had always known that. But it felt good to know someone second that. I learnt about who the 3 were, about their lives, and their journey here. A revolution was on its way. I had just realised how very little I knew about the motive of Dracoros, seeing as I had been focusing on why they had taken my sister. My mind kept wandering off to that, I had come so far, failing now would be a shame and I had nowhere to go. The revolution was hardly 3 weeks away, even less.

They didn't want that to happen, of course, they didn't. The world they had known for a few years wouldn't replace the world they had known for their entire lives. Our paths had been entwined like rope, it had to be a sign. *Life was just a game of truth or dare. Trust people or take risks. Often both.*

We had been walking for a good few hours. I learnt more about them in less than a day than I had learnt about my sister in 13 years. The thing about her left a bitter taste in my tongue and a heaviness in my head that I couldn't explain. We walked ahead, and it felt like me and Erle had a connection. I spoke with her the most, like friends who had known each other their entire lives. I whipped out the map the map maker had made for me. There was around 5 km before the first security checkpoint. There were 3 in total, all of them a few kilometre apart. Kai explained the plan, but I had one of my own. And it was poison. I knew exactly how many officers were stationed outside each checkpoint. I quietly thanked the security camera for how easily it was able to hack. There were 4 guarding this one, 3 in the next one, and 5 in the last. I had brought enough poison to kill a small town, and a small town in this country had at least 200 people. I fingered the little green bottle that I stored the cyanide in. The security received a parcel every morning, made by the kitchen located at one of the corners of the tunnel, and it was transported here in railings on the ceiling, which defied gravity. If they managed to place even a little bit of the food, like the drink or one edge of a bread slice, it would do the job. The excitement made her jittery and anxious, like the morning of your birthday.

We were nearing the security camp, now less than 800m away. The next day, sharp 6, they reached the security camp's region. The tracks began, going through the ceiling leading through the checkpoint and into the kitchen. No one worked there, just a few robots Edwin (one of Erle's friends) had built, with a steady supply of food coming from the main quarters. We had noticed something about the tracks. They weren't railway tracks, but more sticks with hooks that moved. Just ahead, they could see 4 little hay baskets, with the securities' food. I ran ahead, holding the green bottle in one hand. The baskets hadn't yet reached the base, and neither had them, but now was the perfect time to lace the food with poison. I went up to the first one and gasped at the food. The bread was covered in mould, and the apple was half gone, a victim of an insect's hunger. It horrified me. If the cyanide didn't kill them, the mould definitely will. I worked my way through each of the baskets, carefully diluting the cyanide into some juice or mixing it in with some day-old cereal. The cart moved slowly, slower than you could ever imagine. By the time I had finished, the basket hadn't moved a single metre. I wondered how long the basket had taken to reach here. A few hours, or maybe even days? I tried to push it along but it was too heavy. Alok, Erle and Kai tried to help me, slowly pushing each basket towards the checkpoint, following the tracks. It took ages. It nearly takes 3 hours to manually push each basket till almost the very end of the track. There was a large metal gate and behind it was a squat, short building. But this was where everything could go wrong. When the baskets finally touched the end of the track, a soft "DING' was perceived. The basket then fell into the dry, hard mud. One after another, they all fell with a thud. Then came a series of dings after the last basket had fallen. No one came out. We knocked on the metal gate and hid behind a large boulder near it. Still, no one came. My heart started to race. The gate slowly creaked open, and a gust of cold air came out, which was impossible. But many odd things had happened to me, so it wouldn't be a surprise. We walked inside, slowly. My eyes scanned the space, checking if this was a trap. But it wasn't; there wasn't anyone here. There wasn't a single camera, which was confirmed by Kai. It was suspiciously easy to cross the first checkpoint, but our only focus was to get to the

Military Base Camp. If God had made it a little bit easier for us, so be it.

Days had gone by, and we had crossed the second checkpoint. The scenario was the same. I added cyanide to the meals (just in case last time was a one-time occurrence) and pushed it to the checkpoint. The bell rang, and we knocked, yet still, no one was there. This was proving to be easier than I thought. We were nearing the final checkpoint, the most secure one as well. Erle was already preparing the invisibility potion just in case any problems occurred. I still had half a bottle of cyanide left, more than enough for the baskets. Alok was acting odd, odder than when I had first met him. He was quiet but dutiful. His jaw had hollowed out due to malnutrition. It was insane how quickly your body stopped doing as you say when you don't follow what it says. We were a few kilometres away from the 3rd and final security check. After that one, we would be within hours reach of the Military Base Camp, where we all knew where Estella would be. She would have all the answers, and I knew it. Erle had finished making the potion, and there was very little to go around. We used a teaspoon to take a bit of the potion and held it in our mouths. It would take 10 minutes for the potion to take effect and work for 30 minutes. The potion had a sugary, sweet taste. But the aftertaste was horrible, almost bitter and sour. I felt normal after taking it, nothing changed about me. We continue to head towards the security check. I was filled with euphoria and my hands were jittery. I would finally be able to meet my sister after a decade of separation.

This was a jump in my step and a happiness that I hadn't experienced in years. We were nearing the last checkpoint but we had noticed there were no tracks on the ceiling present here. They had stopped a while back, abruptly as if the rest of the tracks had fallen off. I decided not to think much of it, trying to keep hold of this undeserving happiness for as long as possible. My hair was tied up in knots, more tangled than rope. I made a resolution to brush my hair after the security check. I wanted to look half decent when my sister looked at me and saw me grow. The air was starting to get thinner. I felt like I was going up a hill, maybe I was. I couldn't tell which way we were going. The mud walls were beginning to merge again. But I brushed it off as well. Alok was getting more and more quiet, hardly saying a word now. He was a respectful man but was hardly good company. He was the professional sort. I could see how much his brother Guillius resembled him. The same eyes, same facial structure, same emotionless stares. But this man was stronger. He would tear off your bones. His brother was not like that. He was a coward and a freak. He was a Kolispus but showed no signs of it. But he was sweet and gentle. I smiled.

Chapter 21

She was finally going to learn why she was like this, a mistake. When she was taken to the harbour, her ma had whispered "You are not a mistake, you are a miracle." The revolution was now just 18 days away. This was the moment she had been hoping for years on end. To learn why she was like this. Maybe it was a curse, destined to fall upon her. Everything she had thought she had known about Esta was a lie. She wasn't born an Athkarva. She had changed her blood. So why was she, being born into a 100 percent Kolupsis family, an Athkarva?

Chapter 22

We were nearly there. I could see the familiar metal gate right up ahead and sighed. We were finally here. Our guards were low, but we still tried to be as careful as possible. There was no need for the cyanide but the invisibility potions had worked. Right as we were about to slip through the gate, I felt a hand cover my mouth, muffling my scream. How did they see me? I could hear Kai and Erle scream. I couldn't see or hear Alok, but he didn't seem to be captured. The hand across my mouth was from a lady. I looked up at her face, an old woman. But dangerous. Her face was streaked with trauma, her eyes bloodshot and scarlet. Her hair was tied up hastily into braids, and her skin was pale and grey. She took a moment to register my face, her eyebrows shooting up when she saw me in surprise. I didn't think she expected to see the lost princess. Her greying eyebrows twined together in realisation. Her irises dilated, and her breathing got quicker. A harrowing smile marked her face as she stared at one of the guards. "Take the other two away, I'll deal with this one." Kai's lips were a thin line and Alok's rage was evident in his eyes. Erle stared at Juniper, her figure went rigid in fear. I didn't know where they were taking them, but what I didn't know was that I'd find them. The guards took them away, their fingers gripping onto their skin. Now it was just me and Juniper. My father had created charities to fund the search for Juniper, one of the most wanted people in the country. Her face was on Jumbo Trons, flyers, and newspapers. I would expect her to be one of the most advertised women in history. She was a violent lady, her constant wrath and yearning for blood and vengeance made people wary to be near her, fearing for what might come of them if one small thing went wrong. She smirked, one edge of her chapped lips raising. "Why aren't you a pretty little thing?" she whispered in my ear. Dread twisted in my gut. She let her fingers into her pocket and pulled out a syringe. "Handy for situations like this!" she said, in a sick, sweet way. She produced a small vile, from a small brown leather shoulder bag she carried. She carefully poured the liquid in the vial into the syringe, then tapped it twice. "Don't worry princess, this won't hurt a bit." I felt a sharp needle pierce my skin, as a cold rush of liquid filled my blood. It was refreshing and almost cleansing. I could feel my eyes going droopy, and my reflexes sagging. I felt heavier and more stiff. And that was all I could remember.

I woke up with a stinging pain radiating in my arm, my legs were cold and numb. I gently opened my eyes, and the light hit me. I blinked profusely until I finally got adjusted to my surroundings. The wall was built with brick, and the ground was hard cement. The door was to the left of the room, and it was a shiny metal. There was a chandelier hanging up, and storage units, which I assumed were being used to store wine. I must be in a cellar. The ceiling was scattered with security cameras, glaring at me. I wanted to run, but when I tried to get up, I felt something tight and coarse digging against my skin. It must be rope. I didn't like how contained and trapped I felt, like an itch I couldn't reach. I closed my eyes, my mind brimming with questions about my companions. I lay there for about an hour. My stomach was burning from the lack of food. I had no idea how long I had been out for, but it must have been long enough for my last meal to stop giving me any energy whatsoever. Suddenly, I felt the twist of a key and my body filled with quivering excitement. The door creaked open, and I was greeted by someone I assumed was a nurse. She was wearing a pair of pale blue cribs and a white lab coat. Her oily hair was tied up into a half up half down hairstyle and she wore a thin layer of clear lip gloss. She had dark circles underneath her eyes and a face etched with exhaustion. She gave me a slight smile and walked towards me. I began to notice small details about her, like her name tag which suggested her name was Lily Hartling and she wore a light amount of rouge on her cheeks. She rolled up her sleeves and slowly took off the rope that had bound me to the table. There were marks on my skin where the ghost of the rope was, pink and throbbing. She gestured for me to get up. I got up hastily and a wave of pain pierced through me. My legs were sore and they stung. Lily pointed me towards the door, and I limped towards it. She noticed me struggling and lifted my arm over her shoulder trying her best to support me. She used her other hand to open the door and close my eyes so I wouldn't see where we were going. I was brought into another room and I could tell from the creaking of another door. "Hello Princess Aurella Raven" I heard a raspy voice say. My mind clicked. Juniper.

Chapter 23

She fluttered her eyes open. She was bound to the wall with rope and felt some tape placed on her lips. Her eyes scanned her environment. There were many people here, who met with the same fate as her. But none of those faces resembled the princess. She was used to being alone, but the past few days had been more thrilling than she had expected. Being alone wasn't bad as long as you didn't *feel* alone. She couldn't find the coast member either. Her head felt numb and heavy, drooping down. She must've fallen when she got here or banged her head against the wall somehow. Her vision was blurry and unclear. There was a metal door latched up with several locks, confining more than 20 prisoners in one small claustrophobic room. But she was Erle Bloodstone. This wasn't anywhere near as bad as the things she had been through the last couple of years.

She spent the next few hours in a daze. Sleeping and waking up to the hushed chatter of the inmates, exchanging conversations with blatant terror in their eyes and hollowing cheeks. She couldn't end up like them. She wondered where Juniper was, where she had taken the princess. But Erle wasn't foolish. She knew she wouldn't get off easy. She's going to be killed, but she might as well make it worth it. She was going to find out where Estella Raven was, and she was going to find her right now.

Suddenly, she heard the door creak and a jangling of keys from the other side. The prisoners shuffled so they wouldn't be in the way, and their eyes became more livid. Their excitement for the food was undisguised. A tall, blonde woman entered the room, carrying a cart with small plastic plates with tiny portions of food. It looked like a sandwich and some flower fruit. She handed them out to the hungry, desperate prisoners. Erle drank a bit of water, her parched throat yearning for some beverage. It was thicker than honey, with a chlorine taste. The sandwich was dry and stale and the cheese inside of it was mouldy and rubbery. It was hours later when she got the same meal again. It felt like the hours she was waiting for the food started to get longer and longer. Her anticipation for the food increased, and soon she got the same look in her eyes as the other inmates when the food was brought in. The food started tasting better and better, as the hours got longer and for some reason,   the portions got smaller. By the 3rd day, her mind was crowded with thoughts of hunger and desperation.   But she had also noticed something. Every day, one of the inmates was taken by the blonde lady at what she assumed was a little past noon. And they hadn't yet returned. On the 4th day, the blonde lady returned a little past noon, carrying even smaller portions of sandwiches. This time she walked towards her, grabbed her arm, and dragged her out. Erle's consciousness finally returned. This was it. She was going to die. Without ever learning who her "clone" was, or ending Dracoros. Her entire body still ached, and she limped when the woman dragged her. When they were out of the inmate facility, she tied a white handkerchief across her eyes. Erle calculated how many turns she was taking and counted her steps. Finally, she entered a room and heard the door close and the lock click.   Her eyes were her way of acknowledging the world. They were her most powerful tool, and now she was deprived of them. She felt suffocated, and controlled. Finally, the kerchief was taken off her eyes. The freedom was exhilarating. The room she was in was moulding and smelt like moss. It reminded her of the base she was confined to for 3 years. Another 2 ladies came in, bringing in Kai and Alok. One of the ladies had a black eye and a bloodied lip. She would've guessed that was Alok's doing. They were all thrown into the room. The blonde lady finally spoke. "I don't know why you're here, but you won't be going out ever again." She had a thick accent. Erle assumed she was either from the north or the east of the country. Kai's face was clouded with worry, and Alok was quiet and emotionless. They were each handcuffed with cold metal and that rubbed against their skin. There was nothing in the room they were in, no chairs, no food, but a small vent for air. The three ladies left, locking the door on their way out. Erle stared at the coast members. Alok wasn't scared, and it was obvious. "The Coast will realise we're gone. They'll find us," He said. Kai and Erle knew that wasn't true. The level of security here was unimaginable, and they would have no way to track them down. She stared at them with empty eyes, waiting for some sort of conversation to spark. Alok's face was focused, analysing the door. His eyes lit up, and he glanced at Kai. "The bobby pin. Do you still have it?"

He asked in feverish excitement. Kai looked up in confusion, and a faint smile appeared. She nodded then eyed the handcuffs. He glanced at Erle. There was a plan forming now. But they were in one of the most heavily protected quarters of Dracoras, and getting out wouldn't be easy. They had all come here with one goal, finding Estella Raven. To find the truth about her, and perhaps to find some truth about themselves. They were so consumed by Estella's life that it started to become their own. A lingering part of their past, present, and future. For all they could know, she could be in the very same quarters as them.

They had finally come up with a plan. Erle shuffled towards Kai, careful to keep out of sight of cameras and when she was in view, to look innocent and not be suspected of anything. She mouthed "Where's the pin?" Kai looked at her robe pocket. Erle sat down in front of her and reached into her pocket, restricted by the handcuffs. Finally, she managed to fish the bobby pin out. But they had to wait. Or at least a little while until things cooled down. Erle was getting tired of having to leap of faith every time she wanted to live a normal life. She never believed in fate, just luck. Some people assume they're the same. But they're not. Fate is an inevitable force controlled by a higher power. Luck was far simpler, it was uncontrollable and unpredictable.

She had given up on the fact a god was looking upon her, a multiple choice quiz for her life, blindly chosen with have-closed eyes and a finger pointing towards the option. A game of fortune. A game she didn't want to play.

They had been in the room for hours. She was starved of the firm sandwiches and thick water. A food she had now started to have quite the craving for. There wasn't anyone coming in for food, they hadn't seen the 3 ladies since they had left the room after tossing them there. It was hard to believe that just over a week ago, she had been wishing whole-heartedly to see her clone, to find out the truth for herself. But now, it was uncomfortable, knowing she could be anywhere. She had never felt this type of nervousness before. Not once in her life.

Alok was growing increasingly impatient. They had all taken off their handcuffs now but kept them close in case the ladies came back. Alok was also getting thinner. Quicker than Erle and Kai. His violent spirit seemed to have been crushed by these depressing walls. Erle still remembered the way to this room. 20 steps straight ahead, 13 steps left, 4 steps right. Into a corridor which separated into several tiny rooms, which was the only thing she saw with her own eyes and not her legs. This was the 4th room to the right. She wasn't entirely sure how to get out of the quarters completely. She didn't know what to do. Not just now, but for the future. Where would she go, Juniper certainly wouldn't want her back. She could hide in support camps, disguising herself as a homeless or malnourished person. She held onto the tiny spark of hope, that the king would be rejoiced to finally see his daughter and pardon her from her consequences. But every bit of her knew she was being irrational. The Hergal didn't care for the princess. This prompted another thought. They had to find Aurela. Surely the king would be excited to see his only other daughter back home. Maybe Aurela would be her key to freedom. Something she had so desperately wanted for 3 years. But it wouldn't be easy. She knew that. She wasn't unrealistic. But the time had come. The ladies hadn't been back in several hours. However, none of them felt hungry. Now, they couldn't tell how much time had passed. They were each caught in their fever dream, imagining scenarios they knew would never happen. All of them had a goal, a desire they yearned for. Erle so desperately wanted to be normal, a koluspus. Instead of an outcast. More so, she wanted to know why she was like this. What Estella had to do with it. There came Aurella, an escaped princess from a corrupt royal family in a wrecked kingdom. The only person she could talk to was running away when they both were just children. It scarred her, of course, it would. All she cared about now was why. She didn't know why or what. There weren't any questions buzzing around in her head like they usually do, now it was just blank. She just wanted to see her sister again, after all these years. She didn't know what she'd do when she saw her, but that didn't matter. She knew she would figure it out by the time she got there. Alok wasn't sure what he wanted, it was a blur in his head. He didn't want the same things he longed for just a few days ago. He was in a vicious circle of depression and regret, he had lost himself completely. Kai's life was fragmented, as serrated pieces of glass distributed across the floor, eager to be reassembled into the attractive glassware it was before. Each piece of glass grasped one of the answers to her many questions. It would give meaning back to her life, and lift a burden off her shoulders. It was laughable just how much one person could affect many people's lives. Estella was at the heart of their past, present and future. And it was time to get answers.

Chapter 24

I didn't know where she was. Juniper could be an enemy or an ally, but I wouldn't stoop as low to the latter. I knew she was still there, watching over me with her hawk eyes, piercing through my skin like blades of a dagger, leaving wounds marked across my body. It had been so long since I had heard the voice, and for some reason, I wanted to hear it again, I wanted to fight. Time was like a river, constantly flowing forward, carrying us along its currents whether we're aware of it or not. It's both a measurement and a sensation, quantifiable yet elusive.

Sometimes, it seems to drag on endlessly, each moment feeling like an eternity, especially when we're waiting for something eagerly. Other times, it slips through our fingers like grains of sand, leaving us wondering where it all went.

In the dim, flickering light of a subterranean chamber, I pressed my ear against the cold, stone wall, straining to catch any hint of movement from the guards. My heart pounded in my chest, matching the rhythmic dripping of water from the ceiling. The damp air was heavy with the scent of mildew and despair, a constant reminder of the hopelessness that pervaded the underground slave market. For now, I was alone, but I knew Kai, Erle, and Alok were somewhere in this labyrinthine dungeon, where citizens oppressed by this cruel society were taken. The overseers, cloaked in shadow, wielded their power ruthlessly, ensuring that no one ever escaped. But I was determined to defy the odds. The guards' footsteps faded into the distance, and I knew I had to act quickly. I slipped out of my hiding spot, my slender form moving silently through the darkened corridors. The maze-like structure of the underground prison was designed to break the spirit, but my resolve was unyielding. I had overheard whispers of a hidden passageway, an ancient tunnel that led to the surface. It was a risky gamble, but it was my only chance.

Clutching a small, rusted bobbie I had stolen from Kai, I made my way to the iron gate that barred the entrance to the tunnel. My hands trembled as I inserted the bobble into the lock, jarring it in. The gate creaked open, revealing a narrow passage shrouded in darkness. As I ventured deeper, the air grew colder, and the walls closed in around me. The passage twisted and turned, each corner filled with uncertainty. I pressed on, driven by the memory of Kai, Alok and Erle. They had been taken too, I was certain of it, and I would not leave without them. At last, I found myself in another section of the massive headquarters. I soon heard the familiar blaring of security alarms and the blinding red lights that flickered around the corridors, *they were looking for me*. It felt good to be back on the run. That was the only thing she was good at, running away. My breaths came in ragged gasps as I raced through the dimly lit corridors of the underground headquarters, my heart pounding in my chest like a drumbeat of panic. Every shadow seemed to leer at me, every echo of footsteps behind me felt like the approach of doom. I dared not slow my pace, knowing that capture meant a return to the darkness from which I had fought so hard to escape. *I need to find my sister.* Then suddenly, I felt a sharp, excruciating pain in my leg. As the needle pierced my skin, a cold shiver ran down my spine. I felt a fleeting moment of panic, knowing that I was about to lose control over my own body. The liquid flowed into my veins, spreading its numbing tendrils throughout my system. My knees buckled, and I plummeted towards the ground, the world spinning around me in a dizzying blur. The impact was sudden and jarring, sending shockwaves of pain rippling through my body. I struggled to stay conscious, fighting against the overwhelming urge to surrender to the darkness creeping at the edges of my vision.

Every movement felt like wading through molasses, my limbs heavy and unresponsive. I tried to lift myself up, but my muscles refused to cooperate. It was as if I'm trapped in a nightmare, unable to escape the suffocating grasp of sedation.

The world around me blurs and distorts as if seen through a warped lens. Sounds become muffled, distant echoes in the vast emptiness that surrounds me. Despite my best efforts to focus, my mind felt disjointed, and fragmented, as if I'm trapped in a waking nightmare.

Panic clawed at the edges of my consciousness, threatening to overwhelm me with its suffocating grip. But I clung to a fragile thread of awareness, refusing to surrender to the sedative's embrace. With each laboured breath, I fought to maintain control, praying for the strength to endure until the effects began to wane.

In the midst of the chaos, a glimmer of hope flickers within me, a beacon in the darkness. I steel myself for the long and arduous battle ahead, determined to emerge victorious against the numbing tide that threatened to consume me.

Two guards rushed towards me, using brute force to yank me up from my knees. The tears that gathered in my eyes transformed them into shimmering jewels of raw emotion. I couldn't help but to think about where Alok, Erle and Kai were while I was being dragged towards Juniper.

Though our acquaintances were brief, their presence lingers in my mind like a haunting melody I can't seem to forget. Their image is already etched into my thoughts, an indelible mark on my soul despite the short time we've known each other. However, from the moment I laid eyes on Juniper, an unsettling chill ran down my spine. Her features were as unkind as their demeanour: a perpetual scowl carved into a face that seemed to repel any semblance of warmth. Sharp, narrow eyes darted suspiciously, never resting long enough to convey sincerity. Her thin, pursed lips twisted into a sneer more often than not, making every word they spoke drip with disdain. Even her voice had a grating quality, like nails on a chalkboard, each syllable a deliberate attempt to unsettle. My heart hammered in my chest, my breath coming in shallow, panicked gasps. A triumphant smirk twisted across her lips, and her eyes gleamed with a sinister delight that made my blood run cold. "Did you really think you could get away, little princess?" she purred, her voice dripping with mockery. My mind raced, every instinct screaming at me to run, but there was nowhere left to go and my legs had given up. Her presence was suffocating, a dark cloud of menace that seemed to drain the light from the room. With each slow, deliberate step she took toward me, I felt my courage falter, leaving me paralyzed. "You should have known better, there's no knight in shining armour to save you now." she hissed, leaning in close, her breath hot against my ear. Desperation clawed at me as my eyes darted around, searching for any possible escape, but it was clear—there was no evading Juniper's grasp this time. I opened my mouth to reply, but she pulled out one, long and gnarled finger, resembling ancient tree branches twisted by centuries of harsh winds. "I hear from your little friends that you're looking for someone?" My heart dropped, she knew where they were and she was not going to tell me.

I felt a type of rage in my body I had never felt before. Like a red-hot fire burning at the back of my eyes. There were so many things I wanted. I wanted to see my sister again, I wanted to see my newly made friends again, but not for a single moment did I find myself wishing to see my parents once more. At this point, I just wanted it to all be over. I wanted to wake up in the chamber where I had stayed with my sister right beside me. Back when there was nothing between. Not blood or distance. But that was never going to happen. Nothing would change what had happened. It was up to me to make this better. Then I heard a voice, and oh my god. I felt my pain disappear. It felt like a slow wave of relief washing over me. The throbbing sensation that had been dominating my awareness began to fade. I noticed my muscles relaxing, letting go of the tension they've been holding onto. It was like a heavy weight lifting off my body. I knew whose voice this was and it was exhilarating. I looked up, my head light and dizzy. Then I saw her. She had the same face as me. Same soft, thulian pink lips, button nose and eyes that lit up the world. Her strawberry blonde hair tied up into a half up-half down. She looked the same as she had 12 years ago, except her face was sharper, more defined. It had lost its carefree, energetic self. She looked more serious, more mature. But it looked like my own reflection, my presence in another being. My sister. Her voice filled my ears like sickly sweet honey, making me forget every little thing I disliked about her. How she left me to fend for myself in my family, how she betrayed our entire bloodline, how she *corrupted our kingdom*. All my anger, and all my rage buildup over years and years, floated away into the distance. I'd never been so happy and full of ecstasy in my life. "Aurella?" she whispered. "Estella." She smiled a little, and it made my heart flutter, an unmatched happiness.

Chapter 25

We were all in a room nestled deep underground, near the tunnel we had all gone through to reach here. The air was damp and carried a faint scent of mould, rust, and wet soil. Exposed pipes ran along the low ceiling, dripping occasionally and creating small, dirty puddles on the cracked concrete floor. The room was lit by a single, flickering fluorescent bulb, casting harsh, erratic shadows on the stained walls.

In the centre of the room stood a metal table, bolted to the ground, with seven mismatched chairs on either side. The table's surface was scratched and dented, bearing the marks of countless confrontations. One wall was adorned with a large, antique mirror, its surface slightly tarnished, providing a distorted reflection of the room. It was a one-way mirror, behind which unseen observers could watch the proceedings without being detected. It looked just like an interrogation room, and I felt sorry for my sister. She had been in one of these so many times. Trying to clear her name, and prove her innocence and her blood. We all sat in one of the chairs. Juniper in the middle with a spare seat and Kai on either side of her. Across her was Erle on the left, then me and my sister beside her. There were no windows, and the heavy, reinforced door seemed to absorb all sound, making the room eerily silent save for the occasional drip from the ceiling. The walls were lined with shelves holding various tools and instruments, their purposes ambiguous but intimidating. The overall atmosphere was oppressive, designed to unnerve and disorient anyone brought into its depths.

The only indication of the outside world was the faint hum of machinery, reverberating through the pipes and walls, a constant reminder of the subterranean nature of this sinister space. My nails had grown to a quarter of an inch, filled with dirt and mud from clawing through the tunnel for days. I reckoned its earthy, deep scent still lingered on me. Kai looked about the same as she had the first time they had met. Sharp, prominent features, hooded eyes, and near-spotless face. I wondered how she'd done it. Erle aged more in a few days than my sister did in 13 years. Dark circles claimed her under eyes, and her untamed hair sat matted near her shoulders, yearning for a brush. Freckles dotted her face, juxtaposing the rest of her face, almost making her look younger than older. It was the wrinkles above her forehead that sealed the deal. They were rather from worry than age, markings of her fear. The only person missing from this ensemble was Alok. Alok Gaudin. At one point, he was the most feared man of his generation. Now he was just a jumble of nerves and fear. The last time I had seen him, I could distinctly tell the sheer terror in his eyes, reflecting the trauma he'd been through. I wasn't sure where he was, but worry gnawed at me like a relentless insect, its low hum swelling into a roar that drowned out everything else. Juniper sat there, her eyes fuelled by fire, her deep black iris the colour of fire. Her immaculate slicked back hair contrasted the rather chaotic, unexpected situation she had found herself in. She stared at me, her eyes piercing into my skin, burning them like strong acid. She smiled thinly, sending a shiver down my spine, radiating a mad, cruel intensity that made my blood run cold. Yet her unvocal ways of provoking fear didn't distract me from speculating where Alok had been. I turned my head slightly to the left, whispering to Erle, "'"Have you seen Alok?" She shook her head, her face bearing the same worried expression as mine. Juniper smiled wider, and I noticed Esta's body grew tenser. This can't be good. Kai looked visibly uncomfortable, shifting and squirming in her seat like she had pins and needles. Juniper raised her hand, surprising me with her well-maintained nails, making mine look even more deceitful. She clicked them twice, before the large metal door creaked open, casting a shadow from the dim lights and the dark exterior of a familiar figure. I could almost immediately recognise who it was. Alok Gaudin. The man was a sight to behold. His features had become far more aggressive than they used to be, with narrow eyes and a tightly clenched jaw. His muscles were visible even through his loose clothes, his expression intense. Tightly knit eyebrows and a slight scowl on his face, making him appear focused. Despite everything, however, there was a hint of sadness in his stern demeanour. He had a different attire to what I had last seen him in, black button up full arms hurt, rolled up at the elbows, and trousers, with a shiny pair of black shoes. His hair was neatly brushed back and gelled, and the dirt and mud on his face was washed away. This was the first time I had seen him completely clean. There was a slit in between his eyebrow, which I seemed to have never noticed, and a scar that ran along his chin to his cheek. He was being followed by two even larger men, who I assumed were bodyguards. Esta froze, and her eyes widened. All three of them were holding guns, two revolvers and one shotgun. Juniper's mouth widened in pleasure, wearing a full smile. "All four of you brats know too much, so I have no choice but to kill you." I couldn't help but smirk, *one of the most wanted females of our country and she couldn't come up with something less direct.* Kai eyed Alok, her face full of desperation and betrayal. I wanted to reach out, to pull her from the abyss of hurt and confusion, but I knew that only time could heal wounds this deep.

I wasn't the one who betrayed her, but I felt the weight of it all the same. I felt it in the way she looked at me, seeking answers I couldn't provide, solace I couldn't fully offer. How do you comfort someone when the person they trusted most has turned their back on them? I wished I had the power to erase her pain, and rewrite the story with a happier ending.

"I just don't understand," she said, her voice breaking. "How could he do this to me?" I nodded, just as confused as her. I could tell, even by not knowing them for more than 2 weeks, that her connection with Alok was more than just professional. It was friendship.

Something that I could never ever relate to. I wanted to help, I wanted to do something. But all I could manage to say was, "I know." I had never seen my sister more terrified in her whole life. It was as if she knew the power Alok held, the power she didn't have. Juniper finally decided to speak up, "Wow! What a surprise, eh?" She laughed, breaking the cold silence in the room. Alok, let out a low, quiet laugh, a laugh having undertones of fear rather than joy. "This smart lad chose our company rather than death, now wasn't that clever?" Juniper viewed Alok. "And I'm willing to give all 4 of you the very same choice. Would you rather choose our hand or death's hand?" She smiled sweetly, covering her words in fake sickly sweet affection. Erle and Esta gave each other a quick glance. Fear grips me like a vice, squeezing the breath from my lungs. It's an icy chill that starts at the base of my spine and spreads, paralysing my limbs and clouding my thoughts. My heart races, pounding so hard that it feels as though it might burst from my chest. Each beat echoes in my ears, amplifying the silence around me.

My mouth is dry, and I swallow hard, trying to summon some moisture to speak, but the words catch in my throat. My hands are clammy, shaking uncontrollably despite my efforts to steady them. Sweat beads on my forehead, trickling down in cold rivulets that only heighten my sense of dread.

Estella spoke first. Her voice was loud and clear, reflecting off the walls and echoing through the almost empty room. "I'd like to continue my service towards our cause, Juniper." I felt my heart drop. It felt like a knife piercing my chest, a wound that throbbed with a relentless, aching pain. Initially, there was shock—an almost numb disbelief that someone I trusted so deeply could hurt me in such an intimate way. My mind raced, trying to piece together the moments leading up to the betrayal, searching for signs I might have missed, clues that now seemed glaringly obvious. This was Estella. She was leaving me just like she had all those years ago. I didn't know why I was surprised.

As the shock wore off, anger surged, hot and consuming. It burned through my veins, making me want to scream, to lash out, to confront the betrayer and demand answers. How could she? The anger was mixed with sadness, a deep, sorrowful ache that seeped into every part of me.

Estella looked at me, and I felt the same type of pain as I had when she had first disappeared. But this time, she winked. My eyes shot up, I didn't know if I had seen it properly. The subtlest, quickest wink ever. It was so faint I wasn't sure. But I was almost sure I had. I didn't know what she was plotting, but I decided to trust her for one last time. I looked up, my eyes staring right into Juniper's. "I would like to begin my service here too." Juniper beamed, her smile lines on full show. "How lovely, I've got my hands on both the princesses. Now what about the rest of you?" Kai and Erle seemed to have caught on, volunteering just as eagerly. "How absolutely wonderful. We've hardly got a week and a half before the grand show so you might as well take some rest now." Juniper said, her voice clearly showing her excitement. We all stood up, with Alok still pointing the gun to our faces. She made us all follow her to a small room, similar to the room I had been in, except without a table and furniture. "This is just like where we had been," Erle whispered into my ear. Alok handcuffed each of us, before being humbled and being placed in a handcuff himself. Dinner's at 7, and we'll escort you out into the mess hall so no need to worry." Juniper spoke, in a voice you would use to explain simple things to young children. She spoke so slowly, I'm sure it would have reached 7 already. We all mumbled a collection of thank you and saw you soon before she locked the large, cliche metal door behind her. Turning her key to hear a satisfying click. Erle looked visibly astonished with our current circumstances, and I didn't blame her one bit, all of us had been trying to find Estella for years, to complete a part of us. She was the one person who had brought us all together. But it was Erle who had started all this, her knowledge was valuable, it led this search towards the headquarters, it led to me finding my sister. But I knew Kai must have so many questions floating restlessly in her head, her sheer politeness towards me bonding with my sister stopping her from asking them. I looked at her, eyed Esta, and mouthed, "Go on, ask her." Erle grinned. She cleared her throat before looking directly at Estella and speaking, "Are you...my clone?" she whispered. Estella's eyes widened. " Have you been modified too?"

About the author

Sahana is a 13-year-old UK-based young author: an avid reader and a passionate writer, who immensely enjoys every aspect of reading and storytelling. Sahana has always aspired to write and publish her own books and one day become a renowned author.

With this pursuit, she wrote & published her first book, **Witchy Elements**, a fantasy-based fiction, when she was merely 10 years old, and then her second book, **The Robins**, a family comedy & drama, at the age of 11, both published in over 6 countries across the world. Her current work, **Missing Blood**, is yet another fantasy-based fiction, reflecting her deep interest in the genre.

Her quest for reading started at a very young age, and to date, Sahana has read over 600 books and is still counting. Through her books, she hopes to inspire other young readers to experience the real fun and joy of reading in a world where virtual screens are taking over the power of human imagination... by the day. For more details about the author & her work, please visit **www.sahanaravi.com.** Other books from the author (available on Amazon.com).

Story of twin sisters Lisa & Sanchi, who with their magical powers, decode a mystery to save their school from evil powers, with twists and twirls almost in every page.

Story of Allice Robins who navigates her way to happiness in the ten member Robins family, where luck may not have been her friend always, but her charm & wit did.

www.ingramcontent.com/pod-product-compliance
Lightning Source LLC
LaVergne TN
LVHW041854070526
838199LV00045BB/1596